P9-DBZ-710

NORTH CHICAGO
PUBLIC LIBRARY

Flannel Kisses

Flannel Kisses

Linda Crotta Brennan
Illustrated by Mari Takabayashi

E
BRE

NORTH CHICAGO
PUBLIC LIBRARY

Houghton Mifflin Company
Boston 1997

Text copyright © 1997 by Linda Crotta Brennan
Illustrations copyright © 1997 by Mari Takabayashi

All rights reserved.
For information about permission to reproduce selections from this book,
write to Permissions, Houghton Mifflin Company, 215 Park Avenue South,
New York, New York 10003.

For information about this and other Houghton Mifflin trade and reference
books and multimedia products, visit The Bookstore at Houghton Mifflin
on the World Wide Web at http://www.hmco.com/trade/.

The text of this book is set in 24 point Weiss.
The illustrations are watercolor, reproduced in full color.

Library of Congress Cataloging-in-Publication Data
Brennan, Linda Crotta.
Flannel kisses / by Linda Crotta Brennan;
illustrated by Mari Takabayashi.
p.   cm.
Summary: Rhyming text describes a winter day spent playing in the snow.
ISBN 0-395-73681-1
[1. Snow — Fiction.   2. Play — Fiction.   3. Winter — Fiction.   4. Stories in rhyme.]
I. Takabayashi, Mari, 1960 – ill.   II. Title.
PZ8.3.B7455F1   1997 [E] — dc20   96-2997   CIP   AC

Manufactured in the United States of America
BVG   10 9 8 7 6 5 4 3 2 1

For my husband, who warms me with his flannel kisses.
— L.C.B.

For my husband, Kam, and our daughter, Luca.
— M.T.

Flannel sheets,
Cold floor,

Hot oatmeal,

Out the door!

Slippery snowsuit,
Sticky snow,

Pack a snowball,

Make it grow.

Pile snowballs,

Small on fat.

Crown icy head
With fuzzy hat.

Dry socks,
Soup's best.

Red nose rubs

Dad's flannel chest.

Back outside,

Dig snowy square,

NORTH CHICAGO
PUBLIC LIBRARY

Stove and table,
Hard-packed chair.

Toes cold,
Cheeks red,

Smell hot stew,

Baking bread.

Fireside story,

Say good night,

Flannel kisses
By pale starlight.